PEANUTS®

No Rest for the EASTER BEAGLE

by Charles M. Schulz
adapted by Tina Gallo
illustrated by Scott Jeralds

Ready-to-Read

Simon Spotlight

New York   London   Toronto   Sydney   New Delhi

SIMON SPOTLIGHT
An imprint of Simon & Schuster Children's Publishing Division
1230 Avenue of the Americas, New York, New York 10020
This Simon Spotlight edition January 2020
© 2020 Peanuts Worldwide LLC
All rights reserved, including the right of reproduction in whole or in part in any form.
SIMON SPOTLIGHT, READY-TO-READ, and colophon are registered trademarks of Simon & Schuster, Inc.
For information about special discounts for bulk purchases, please contact Simon & Schuster Special Sales at
1-866-506-1949 or business@simonandschuster.com.
Manufactured in the United States of America 1219 LAK
2 4 6 8 10 9 7 5 3 1
ISBN 978-1-5344-5480-4 (hc)
ISBN 978-1-5344-5479-8 (pbk)
ISBN 978-1-5344-5481-1 (eBook)

It is almost Easter.
Everyone is excited.
Everyone, that is, except
the Easter Beagle.

Charlie Brown brings Snoopy his
food.
"You look terrible, Snoopy," he
says.
"You need to rest!"
Snoopy shakes his head.
He doesn't have time to rest.

There is still so much to do!
There are still so many eggs
to be colored.
Then all the eggs need to be
hidden.
How will Snoopy get it all
done in time?

Snoopy tries to hurry.
He is painting the eggs so fast,
his paintbrush breaks.
Snoopy is upset.
He knocks a dozen eggs
onto the floor.

"Let's go talk to Lucy,"
Charlie Brown says.
"Maybe she'll know what to do."

Charlie Brown and Snoopy
visit Lucy at her booth.
"Snoopy, you're exhausted,"
Lucy says.
"I think you need to take a
break from Easter this year."

Snoopy nods his head.
He loves Easter, but he
needs to rest!
"We need someone to
deliver the eggs," Lucy
says.

"I can deliver the eggs,"
Charlie Brown says.
"As I was saying, we need
somebody really great to deliver
the eggs," Lucy replies.

Everyone wants to help!
But there are problems.
Woodstock can't lift the basket.
Pigpen is too messy.

Sally keeps writing about her love for her "Sweet Babboo" on all the eggs.

Linus has to recolor
all the eggs Sally
has written on.

Rerun wants the eggs to be
perfect.
He studies every single egg and
keeps adding decorations.
He will never get around
to delivering them.

Peppermint Patty keeps
pitching the eggs to Marcie,
who can't catch them.
They end up breaking all the eggs!
Schroeder just paints music notes
on all his eggs.

Lucy is sad, but she decides
she must cancel the Easter
egg hunt.
"We have no choice," she
tells Charlie Brown.

"Snoopy is still so tired.
Maybe he'll feel better in time
to be the Flag Day Beagle!"

Charlie Brown finds Snoopy
and Woodstock asleep on top
of Snoopy's doghouse.
"We are canceling the
Easter egg hunt," Charlie Brown
tells them.

Snoopy is surprised.
*I thought someone else would
take over*, Snoopy thinks.

Everyone looks sad
and disappointed.
"I know it's a lot of work, Snoopy,"
Charlie Brown says.
"But no one can save the
Easter egg hunt but you!"

Snoopy looks at Woodstock
and smiles.
This is a job for the Easter Beagle!
he thinks.

Snoopy knows he still needs help.
So he gathers his friends together.
He gives them all jobs to do.

Woodstock will decorate the eggs.
He has the perfect light touch.

Peppermint Patty and Marcie will pack the eggs in the Easter basket.

Schroeder will take the Easter
basket to Lucy.
Lucy will give the Easter basket
to Linus and Sally.

Linus and Sally will
hide the eggs.

Pigpen will stand and be
the lookout.
He will make sure nobody sees
where the eggs are hidden.

Easter is finally here!

Everyone has a great time finding all the beautiful Easter eggs.

Charlie Brown looks and looks.
He doesn't find a single egg!
And the Easter Beagle has none
left to give him.

"That's okay, Snoopy," Charlie
Brown tells him.
"I'm just happy you saved the day!"

Suddenly Snoopy surprises
Charlie Brown with a little
American flag!
Lucy laughs.
"Happy Flag Day, Charlie Brown!"
she says.